# Bill the Warthog MYSTERIES

## GUARDING THE
## TABLETS OF STONE

**LEGACY PRESS**®
www.LegacyPressKids.com

Read more about your favorite tusked detective in these Bill the Warthog Mysteries:

**Book 1**
Full Metal Trench Coat

**Book 2**
Guarding the Tablets of Stone

**Book 3**
Attack of the Mutant Fruit

**Book 4**
Quest for the Temple of Truth

**Book 5**
The Bogus Mind Machine

**Book 6**
King Con

**Book 7**
The Case of the Campfire Caper

**Book 8**
Box Office Bill

**Book 9**
Battle of the Bands

# Bill the Warthog
## MYSTERIES

## GUARDING THE
# TABLETS OF STONE

### Dean A. Anderson

*To the folks at Felton Bible Church that made it possible for me to write this.*

*And to the Watsons: Steve, Gwynne, Greg, and Katie (a much more honest Katie than the one in these pages) who kept these stories alive.*

BILL THE WARTHOG MYSTERIES: GUARDING THE TABLETS OF STONE
©2014 by Dean Anderson, ninth printing
ISBN 10: 1-58411-073-2
ISBN 13: 978-1-58411-073-6
Legacy reorder# LP48302
JUVENILE FICTION / Religious / Christian

Legacy Press
P.O. Box 261129
San Diego, CA  92196
www.LegacyPressKids.com

Cover and Interior Illustrator: Dave Carleson

Scriptures are from the *Holy Bible: New International Version* (North American Edition), ©1973, 1978, 1984 by the International Bible Society. Used by permission of Zondervan Bible Publishers.

*Printed in the United States of America*

# Table Of Contents

# The Case of the Vanishing Video Game

Some of you reading this know who I am because you've read other stories about me and my warthog detective friend, Bill. I know this because you've asked me questions like "How did you and Bill meet?" and "Where did you and Bill meet?" and "When did you and Bill meet?"

Because I get asked the same questions again and again, I thought I would write out my answer once and for all, so here's the story.

My name is Nick "Ten Toes" Sayga. Watch me play video games and you'll see why my nickname is "Ten Toes" – I play video games with my feet! I had to learn to work the controls with my feet because it's the only

7

way my friends would take me on. When I played with my hands, I always used to beat them. Winning was cool, but eventually no one wanted to play against me. My feet against their hands seemed to even up the score a bit.

Why am I telling you all this? Because it was a video game that brought Bill and me together.

Most nights after homework and dinner, I play video games. The week I met Bill, I was way into playing "Big Green Slime Time," fighting space monsters with a garden hose.

On Monday night of that week, I sat down to play, but when the first slime monster came on the screen, the lights went out. The power was off for about fifteen minutes.

By the time the power came back on, it was time for bed. So I put on my socks and headed upstairs.

Tuesday night the same thing happened. And Wednesday and Thursday. This was too weird, so I decided I needed to do something about it.

After school that Friday, I looked in the phone book under "Investigators." I called the first number: AAA Private Investigators.

But they wouldn't take my case. So I kept scrolling

down the list until I'd called nearly every detective agency in town. No luck. They all said either that I was too young, being only eleven, or that I didn't have enough money with only $18.94 in the bank.

That is, until I called the last number in the book: Warthog Investigations/William T. Warthog, Owner.

So far I had only talked to receptionists, but this time I heard a deep, peculiar voice: "Good afternoon. Warthog Investigations. Bill the Warthog speaking."

I told Bill my story about how the power kept going out when I tried to play video games. I also told him I was a kid without money.

He assured me he specialized in kids' cases, that I didn't need to worry about money, and that if it was okay with my parents, he'd come right over.

It was raining hard that afternoon, but Bill was at the door in less than an hour. I was surprised that he really was a warthog. I thought it was just a name, like Jack Sparrow.

But there at the door was a real warthog standing upright. He had a long snout on his hairy face, and tusks that seemed to form a large smile.

"Good to meet you, Nick," he said. "Mind if I come in and sit down? Walking on my hind legs wears me out."

I bombarded him with the same questions you would ask.

"How did a warthog learn to talk?"

"How did you become a detective?"

"Why are you wearing clothes?"

He listened politely, but he only answered the last question: "When I walk down the street in my trench coat and hat, fewer people stare at me. And it cuts down on the calls to animal control."

Bill wasn't ignoring my other questions, he was just eager to get on with the investigation. He said I'd have to wait to hear more of his story until he solved my case. And so, I guess, will you.

Bill asked me to tell my story again about the video games and the power outages. I told him my dad didn't think there was anything wrong with our fuse box, and that the other houses in the neighborhood weren't losing power.

"We'll need to do a stakeout," he said when I finished my story.

"What's a stakeout?" I asked.

"That's where we sit and wait to see who's doing

11

this thing," Bill said as he got up to leave.

So that night, at the usual time, I sat down to play. And after five minutes, the lights went out.

But this time, Bill was watching the fuse box. A figure had approached the box in the darkness, opened it and flicked a switch. As Bill drew near, the person ran.

Bill stopped to turn the power back on. He thought he saw a kid run across the street and around to the back of a house. He heard a door slam.

I went outside, and Bill asked me to join him. We crossed the street.

"That's the Smiths' house," I said.

"Any kids live there?" Bill asked.

"Yeah, Hurley lives there. He's about my age."

Hurley came to the door immediately when we rang the doorbell. He invited Bill and me inside, although he kept giving Bill very funny looks. Bill was looking at Hurley's shoes.

"I can't help but notice your muddy feet, Hurley. Were you just outside?"

"Yeah, I was," Hurley responded quickly. "The power went off in our house about a half an hour ago. I waited around for awhile, then tried to call the power company, but our phone doesn't work when the power's out.

"So I went outside to check our fuse box, and then I noticed the power was back on, so I came back inside."

"Hurley, do you have a video game system?" Bill asked.

"No, I wanted a game like Nick's, but my parents said it would be a waste of time and money. They think it's better to spend money on educational supplies. Do you want to see the *Encyclopedia Britannica* I got for my birthday?"

"I don't think so," Bill said. "I see by the digital clock on the shelf there that it's Nick's bedtime, so we really should be going. But before we do, it's also time, Hurley, for you to consider one of the Ten Commandments. The last one.

"And it's time for you to tell us what you were really doing tonight and the last several nights. Because you haven't been telling us the truth."

Why didn't Bill believe Hurley's story? And what is the last of the Ten Commandments, and what could it have to do with this story?

☞ Turn to page 90 to find out!

# Chapter 2

# The Case of the Too-Good-to-Be-True Travels

I stared a bit at the Empire State Building, a skyscraper in New York City. Then I turned and looked at the Swiss Alps.

"Ili, Nick," said Tito, who was standing in front of the Hawaiian Islands poster, as he hung up the phone. "Thanks for meeting me here."

"Here" was the Slight Travel Office. Tito helped his aunt, Mrs. Slight, by answering phones and filing travel brochures.

"No problem, Tito. Did you want to talk about the camping trip?"

"I'm not so sure there's going to be a camping trip," Tito said glumly.

"Why not, Tito? You've been working for weeks on planning this trip. Everyone in the school travel club is looking forward to it. Don't you already have reservations with the state park?"

"Yeah, but if Katie Bartlett wins the election for travel club president, we'll go on the trips she wants to do. Which would be okay, but I'm not sure we'll actually be able to take any of the cool trips she's talking about in her campaign."

"Are you saying you're not sure she's being honest?" I asked.

"Well, Katie's talking about trips to amusement parks in other states, and going to Hawaii and Alaska and even other countries. And she's saying we won't have to pay more to do these trips, just have a few more bake sales. Who wants to go on my dumb old trip to General Grove Falls State Park, Nick, when they can go to Egypt and unwrap a mummy?"

"Tito, the camping trip will be great," I said as I pondered what it might be like to unwrap a real mummy. "All your trips are great. And we both know that parents aren't going to let sixth-graders go by

17

themselves on a weekend trip to Egypt anyway."

Tito nodded his head. "You know there's no way we can afford to do the trips Katie is talking about, and I know it, but how can we prove it?"

"I think I know someone who can help, Tito."

"Someone who goes to our school?"

"I don't think he's ever gone to school, but I do think he'll help."

Bill the Warthog wouldn't take my money when he solved the video game case. He just asked for two things.

First, he asked if he could graze on my front and back yards. Since this meant less lawn mowing for me, I gladly agreed.

Second, he said he could use an assistant. I asked him what that would involve. He said for now I should just keep my eyes and ears open for some interesting cases.

When I called Bill, he thought Tito's case was interesting.

People stared, of course, when we brought Bill the Warthog into the meeting of the Elm Street

Elementary School Travel Club. I think people thought he was there to promote a trip to the zoo. (Even though the animals at your average zoo do not wear fedoras on their heads!)

But when Tito made his speech, promising to do his best to continue offering a program of nearby points of interest at moderate prices, he made no mention of the warthog in the back corner of the room.

Then Katie got up to speak. "Good afternoon, girls, guys, and whatever that thing in the corner is."

I could tell Bill wanted to say something to defend himself, but he held his tongue.

"First of all, I'd like to say Tito Rodriguez did a really good job this last year as travel club president. He planned some nice trips to nice places. But I think we can do better.

"For instance, last month when we had that Friday off school, I went with my father to Paris, France, for the weekend. My father is a pilot, so we get to fly for free.

"We left early in the morning so we could have lunch in New York City. We then took a supersonic jet that goes from New York to Paris in only four hours. We arrived in time for a 6 p.m. dinner."

Katie held up some framed pictures. "I enlarged some photos from that weekend. I went to an art museum called the Louvre, and they let me hold a famous painting."

Katie walked around so kids could see the photo of her holding the Mona Lisa. In the picture, the top of the painting's frame touched Katie's chin and the bottom of the frame sat on her toes.

"And here is a picture of me in front of the famous Eiffel Tower.

"Finally, here is a picture of me by the Notre Dame Cathedral. I love the Hunchback story, so I insisted on going to the cathedral to lay flowers by his grave marker."

Katie slid the pictures back into her backpack. "It was a great trip," she said. "But it would have been even better if I'd had my friends from the travel club along. And next time you will be. I have a plan to take you to all the wonderful sites of the world! That's why you should vote for me as travel club president. Any questions?"

I wished I had a camera to capture the shock on Katie's face when Bill raised a front hoof. Her expression was even better when Bill spoke.

"I have a question. Why do you think anyone would vote for you when I can prove that you didn't tell the truth about your trip to Paris? I really think it's about time you tell the truth, and start honoring the ninth commandment."

What did Katie say that Bill could prove was not true? And what is the ninth commandment?

 **Turn to page 92 to find out!**

# Chapter 3

# The Case of the Quiz Show Questions

"Let's see, it wasn't Abraham Lincoln – they made jokes about him being skinny. Washington couldn't have eaten that much with wooden teeth. I've seen Jimmy Carter on TV – he has good teeth, but he isn't all that big.

"I'd have to go with William Taft as the heaviest President," Thor Swanson said as he leaned into the microphone.

"When he left office, Taft weighed 340 pounds – making you correct, Thor. Congratulations, you win our game and twenty dollars credit at the school snack bar! 'Til tomorrow, this is Skip Burpall with

'Who Wants to Be a Burrito-aire?'"

I had to hand it to Skip. He had made the school's morning announcements on the P.A. system more interesting with his game show. Skip's a fifth-grader in the audio-visual club who came up with the idea of a game show to encourage students to be interested in different subjects.

The school honor society had a drawing for the five students who would compete over five days. The students knew they'd be on the show, but didn't know their day or topic until they were pulled out of class at the beginning of the day, just before the show.

Monday had been math, Tuesday was science, and Wednesday was literature. Thor had played on Thursday when the topic was history. The next day was going to be spelling, the only subject remaining.

I was surprised when Skip approached me at recess. "Hey, Nick," he called out. "Do you really know a pig detective?"

"Actually, he's a warthog," I said. "Why are you asking?"

"Because I think someone is cheating at the game."

Skip told me the story. He had written the questions and answers to his quiz in a notebook that he kept in

his locker. Then he put his final copy of the questions on 3" x 5" cards that he took to the office's public address system each morning.

"Anyway," Skip said, "When I went to my locker after today's game, I saw that the locker had been broken into. And the questions and answers for today and tomorrow had been swiped."

"So who do you think did it?" I asked.

"Well, I think it was obviously Thor, since he did the quiz today, or Cody Fargo, who's scheduled to go tomorrow. I asked both of them to meet me at the principal's office at lunch. I don't want to get them both in trouble, though, if one isn't guilty."

"Okay, Skip. I'll call Bill and see if he can meet us outside of the principal's office at noon. Maybe he can figure this all out."

It took a little talking to get Bill to come. He thought we were meeting in the principal's office rather than outside of it. Principals' offices are right up there with the dentist and a funeral home as places you'd rather not go if you don't have to.

I met Bill in the parking lot, and we found Skip, Thor and Cody waiting outside the office. After I introduced everyone to Bill, Skip unexpectedly apologized.

"I think you've come here for nothing, Mr. Warthog. Tell him what you found, Cody."

"I'm sorry to have to rat on you, Thor," said Cody. "But I saw you throw something in the trash at recess today. So I walked over and pulled this out."

Cody took a crumpled piece of paper out of his pocket. On it were the questions and answers for the history quiz.

"That's not true, Cody! I didn't cheat!" Thor shouted. He shouted so loudly that Mrs. Newberry, Principal Kingstone's secretary, stuck her head out the door.

"Keep it quiet, kids," she said. Then she looked Bill up and down. "Say, I haven't seen you before. What's your name?"

"Ah, um, me?" Bill stammered. "Bill."

"My, it looks like you may need to shave any time now." She went back in.

I explained to Bill that Mrs. Newberry was a little near-sighted (and had fortunately left her glasses in her office).

"Now where were we?" Skip asked.

"Thor was accusing me of lying," Cody said.

"Well, I didn't say that exactly. But I didn't have the answers, and you didn't see me throw them away," Thor said.

"This case is far from being solved, Skip," Bill said. "Either of these two could be lying."

"Well, it's not me," said Cody. "The two subjects are history and spelling, and I never need help with either of those."

Bill looked thoughtful. "Skip, do you have the questions and answers for tomorrow's spelling quiz?"

"Yeah, on a card. Here you are," said Skip as he handed the card to Bill.

Bill looked at Thor and Cody. "Would you both be willing to take this test?"

"I'd rather not," said Thor. "Spelling is not my best subject."

"I'll take it," said Cody. "We'll clear this right up when you see what a great speller I am."

"All right," Bill said. "I'll ask a vocabulary question and then you spell out the word. Here's the first: 'What object on the wall keeps time?'"

Cody smiled. "A clock. C-L-O-C-K."

"Very good," said Bill. "Here's the next question: 'What might a teacher write on a paper if you didn't

finish the work?'"

"Let me think," said Cody. "That would be 'incomplete.' I-N-C-O-M-P-L-E-T-E."

"Well, I'm impressed," said Bill. "In fact, to move along more quickly, I won't even bother with the vocabulary question, I'll just give you the word. Okay?"

Cody nodded.

"Cody, please spell 'stationery.'"

"Stationery? S-T-A-T-I-O-N-E-R-Y."

"Good, how about 'principle'?"

"Principle, P-R-I-N-C-I-P-L-E, principle."

"Here is the last word, Cody. Larceny.'"

"Larceny, L-A-R-C-E-N-Y, larceny. Well, did I get everything right, Mr. Warthog?"

"I'm afraid you did, Cody. You spelled the words exactly as they are on the answer sheet. And only the last word on the spelling sheet can explain how you could do that."

"What are you talking about?" Cody asked.

"I'm talking about the eighth commandment…and about where you have to go next."

"Where do you think I have to go?"

"Into the principal's office, Cody."

How did Bill know that Cody was guilty? What exactly does that last spelling word mean? And what is the eighth commandment?

 Turn to page 94 to find out!

# Chapter 4

# The Case of the Multiplying Pets

I was eager for Daisy to meet Bill. It seemed like they might have some things in common. And I really wanted to know if Bill could translate dog language for me.

So on Saturday, I took Daisy to Bill's office to answer that very question.

"Of course I don't speak dog," Bill sniffed. "Would I bring a German person to you and ask you to translate?"

Daisy seemed to like Bill, because she kept jumping on him. Bill seemed to like Daisy not so much.

"So when did you get a dog?" Bill asked.

"Well, there is an interesting story to that," I said, which pleased Bill. He likes stories, so I told him this one.

About a month ago, my neighbor, Danielle Holbrook, came home from school to find a kitten in a basket on her front porch.

Danielle got a bowl of milk for the kitten, and the kitten lapped it up. When Danielle's mom got home from shopping, Danielle asked if she could keep the kitten. Her mom told her to wait until her father got home.

When Danielle's dad got home from work, her parents talked, then they told Danielle she could keep the kitten.

Danielle told her parents she planned to name the kitten "Princess." But after her mother looked the kitten over, Danielle agreed "King" was a better name.

Then a couple of weeks ago, Danielle found a puppy tied to her porch. Her parents told Danielle she could not have a new puppy along with the new kitten. Danielle remembered we were looking for a dog, so she brought the puppy over.

I wanted to name her "Mario" or "Sonic," but Mom said she needed a girl's name. Dad backed her up on that, and so "Daisy" it was.

Bill asked another question. "Have any more pets appeared on Danielle's porch?"

"Funny you should ask," I said. "Just today, Danielle came back from a sleepover and found a hamster rolling around her front porch in one of those plastic balls."

"Really," Bill said. "I think we should pay Danielle a visit."

Danielle seemed happy to see us. King did not. I don't know if it was Bill, Daisy or me, but when he saw us coming, he dashed into the house.

Danielle didn't know much about warthogs, so I had to assure her he wouldn't eat her kitten or hamster. (Bill told me later that some warthogs do eat small rodents. I was glad he hadn't brought that up in front of Danielle.)

Bill wanted to hear the story of the pets again, so Danielle told him how King the cat, Daisy the dog and the hamster in the ball all appeared on her front porch. Bill asked her if there was a pet shop nearby.

"Yes, there is," Danielle said. "Two blocks down the street. Why do you ask?"

"Would you like us to deal with this hamster?" Bill asked.

Danielle looked at Bill suspiciously.

"I'll look after it," I said.

Danielle nodded.

We went to Noah's Pet Store. Ben, a kid from my school, was behind the counter. It was his father's shop.

Ben was surprised to see someone with so much fur outside of a cage, but he was interested in our story about Danielle's pets.

After I finished telling what happened, Ben took the hamster out of the ball and looked it over. "This hamster looks familiar," he said, "Notice this horseshoe pattern on its back?"

"Where did you see it before?" Bill asked.

"It was in this shop. A kid bought it about a week ago. I think his name was Dennis."

"Do you know how I can get ahold of Dennis?" Bill asked.

"He'll be back here in a few minutes," Ben said as he glanced at the clock. "He just bought a lizard. He's

36

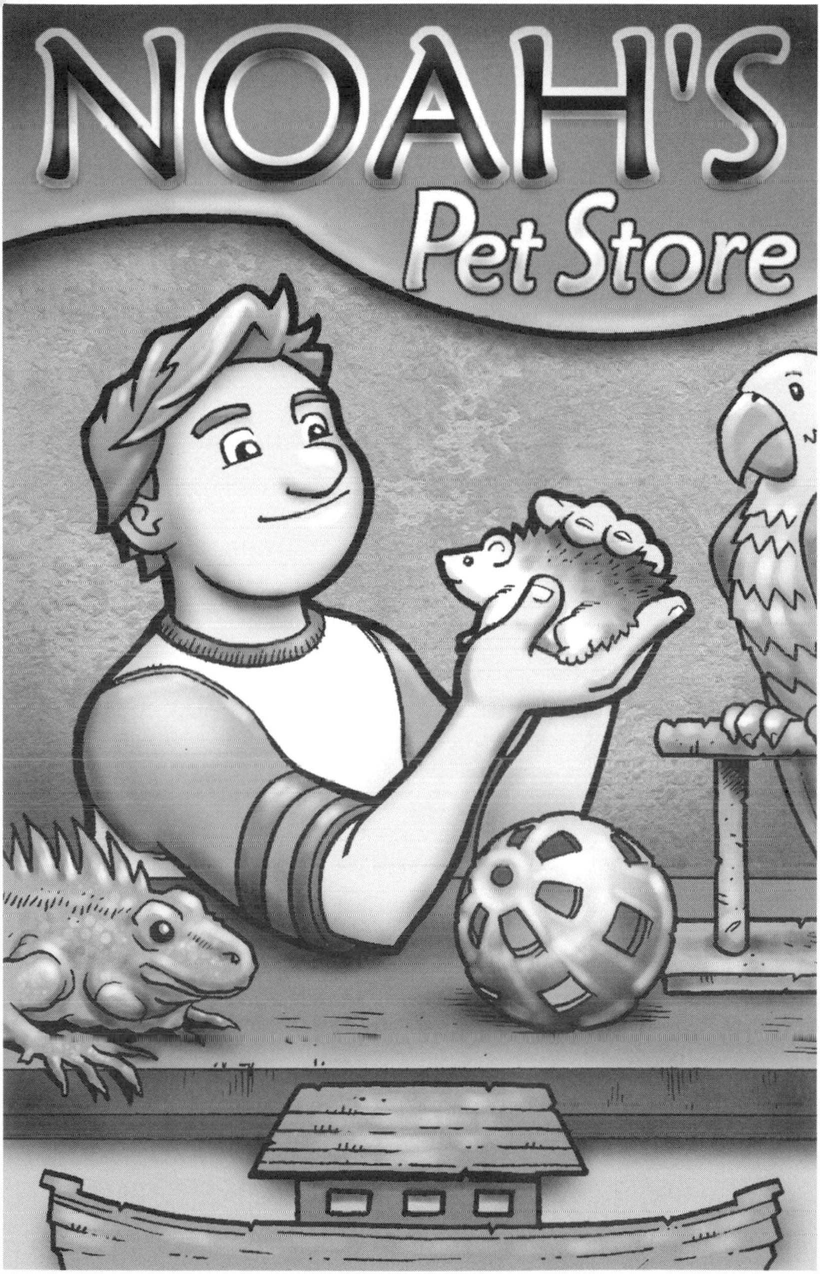
NOAH'S
Pet Store

already paid for it. Said he was going to do some shopping and pick it up later. Should be any time now."

Bill thought for a moment. "Did this Dennis buy a puppy or kitten here recently?"

"We don't sell dogs or cats. But he did buy cat food and supplies a few weeks ago, and then dog stuff a couple of weeks later."

Bill thanked Ben for his help, then he asked me to wait with him in front of the store.

A blonde kid was heading for the store door, but Bill blocked his way. "Are you Dennis?"

"Yeah," the kid said. "What's it to ya?"

"My name is Bill the Warthog, and I'm a private investigator working on a case."

"A detective?" Dennis asked with excitement. "Like on TV? Cool. Are you investigating a robbery or a murder?"

"It's a different kind of case. Dennis, did you buy a hamster a week ago and leave it today on Danielle Holbrook's porch?"

"Um, no. I mean, I bought a hamster last week, but it was a birthday present for my cousin. I gave it to him on Friday."

"Dennis, someone left a puppy on Danielle's porch."

"I didn't leave her there," Dennis said.

"Dennis, did you abandon a kitten on Danielle's porch?"

"He wasn't my kitten, okay? Why are you bothering me?"

Bill shook his head and said, "Because your answers tell me that those were your pets, Dennis. And if you don't learn more about commitment and responsibility, even with pets, you will probably have a real problem with the seventh commandment when you grow up."

How was Bill sure the pets belonged to Dennis? And what is the seventh commandment?

 **Turn to page 96 to find out!**

# Chapter 5

# The Case of the Raccoon Twins

I dropped by Bill's office one Saturday morning. He looked very tired. When I asked him what was up, he told me this story:

I didn't sleep real well. I think I had too much root beer and cricket pizza last night. I fell asleep in front of the TV with an old detective movie playing.

I had the strangest dream. I lived in a world where all the animals talked.

In my dream, I was in my office. My hooves were up on the desk, and I was tilting back in my chair, wondering why I was dreaming in black and white rather than in color. There was a knock at my door.

I called, "Come in," and in came a fox. Really, she was a fox. Her tail was long and shiny, and her eyes were quick and bright. One look at her explained why human beings used her species to describe an attractive person (and why you don't say, "What a warthog!").

"My name is Thelma Fox," she said. "And I'm in trouble."

"Trouble is why people usually come in my door," I answered suavely. "What kind of trouble?"

"Actually, Mr. Warthog…"

"Please, call me Bill, Miss Fox."

"And you can call me Thelma. Actually, it's my father, Stanford Fox, who's in trouble. He's been accused of murder."

"Murder?" I gasped. "Who do they say he killed?"

"An opossum by the name of Percy."

My mind raced. "Are you sure it was Percy Opossum?"

She nodded.

"He's a good friend of mine," I said as I got up. "Come with me to the police station."

When we arrived at the police station, the

receptionist, a yellow-bellied marmot named Lucy, said the body was downstairs.

I went downstairs and saw Percy's body stretched out on the table. I whispered in his ear, "Percy, are you dead or just playing?"

"Bill, is that you?" Percy Opossum asked as he sat up on the table. Thelma Fox screamed.

"Percy, I know you were just pretending to be dead, but this is serious," I said. "This young fox's father was accused of killing you. You've gotten him into real trouble."

"But Bill, someone did try to kill me," Percy said. "Last night, I was at the Raccoon Brothers Pizza Parlor. The song 'It's a Small World' was on the jukebox, and I love that song. So I kept putting in quarters so I could listen to it again and again. The guys were complaining, but I kept playing it anyway."

"Who was at the pizza parlor?" I asked.

"Well, there was this fox," he said as he nodded at Thelma, "and her father, I guess. And, of course, the Raccoon Brothers: Ralph and Roscoe. Oh, and there was a wolverine there. That was all."

"Then what happened?"

"I wanted to play the song one more time. But

someone behind me shouted, 'Don't you dare!' I put a quarter in anyway. Then someone threw a chair at my head.

"I fainted, and then found myself here on this table. So I decided to take a nap. This is a pretty comfortable morgue table."

I turned to Thelma. "Well, at least we know there wasn't a murder, so they should be releasing your father."

"We will be doing no such thing. There may not have been a murder, but there was an attempted murder. So Stanford Fox will be staying, and you will be leaving, Warthog.'

It was the voice I least wanted to hear: Sergeant Burt Weasel. If he was the officer in charge of the case, we were in trouble.

Sergeant Weasel didn't like foxes, for no good reason. He also didn't like me, because he'd put too many innocent people in jail that I'd gotten out. And the Weasel didn't like to be proved wrong.

"Hello, Sergeant Weasel," I said. "I'm here on behalf of my clients, Thelma and Stanford Fox. How do we know it wasn't the wolverine or one of the Raccoons who threw that chair?"

"Oh, it wasn't Ralph or Roscoe," Percy piped up. "I could see them both over the serving counter when the chair came flying."

Thelma broke in. "Then the Raccoon brothers can testify that the wolverine threw the chair."

Sergeant Weasel snarled, "Apparently you don't know that Hugh Wolverine is an upstanding citizen and my friend. I don't like to arrest my friends."

Weasel looked at me. "And this fox doesn't seem to know an important fact about the Raccoon Brothers, does she, Warthog?"

"Bill, what does he mean about the Raccoon Brothers?" asked Thelma.

"Ralph and Roscoe are identical twins," I said. "No one can tell them apart. But they have this quirk: one of 'em always tells the truth, always. And one of them always lies, always."

"That's the truth," said Sergeant Weasel with glee. "We have them upstairs for questioning. One of them says the wolverine threw the chair and the other says the fox threw the chair. I'm inclined to believe it was the fox."

"Perhaps I could help with the questioning?" I asked.

"Do you really think I need your help, Warthog? Do you think you're smarter than me?" Sargeant Weasel growled.

"I do think you need my help," I said proudly. "And I'm not only smarter than you are, I've eaten meal worms that are smarter than you!"

"All right, wise guy. I'll let you talk to the Raccoons. But you get to ask just one question to one Raccoon, got it?"

"Oh, Bill," Thelma fretted, "won't it take several questions just to find out if you're talking to the lying or the truthful raccoon? And then you won't be able to ask who threw the chair."

Then I woke up. But I knew what question I would ask the Raccoons to find out who threw the chair. I also knew whether the wolverine or the fox had tried to break the sixth commandment. And I knew that in the broadest sense, I had broken it in my dream, too.

What question could Bill have asked to solve the mystery? What is the sixth commandment, and what did Bill mean by saying he had broken it in the "broadest sense"?

 Turn to page 98 to find out!

# Chapter 6

# The Case of the Space Mask

Sometimes Bill was bothered by the way clients reacted when they saw him. Occasionally they stared, or laughed, or even screamed. In this case, that wasn't a problem, because Bill never met his client.

Colin, his client, never saw Bill throughout the case. And Bill only saw Colin on TV, or he thought he did. But I'm getting ahead of the story.

One day at recess, I was playing tetherball with Colin Fredricks when a very excited Alex Hampton approached us.

"Hey, Nick! Colin! Did you hear that Marv Martin, Slugtop himself from Space Stuff, is going to be at the

Acme Comic Book Store today?"

You've probably heard of the sci-fi TV series Space Stuff, so I don't need to tell you about the arch villain giant space slug, Slugtop, or the actor who plays him. I haven't seen the show myself (it's on after my bedtime), but lots of kids at my school like it.

"He's going to be there at 3:00! The first hundred people get a free Space Stuff comic and an autographed picture of Marv Martin in his Slugtop costume."

"Man, I wish I could go," said Colin. And I knew he did, because Colin loves anything to do with space. He always talks about how he wants to be an astronaut when he grows up.

"Why do you just *wish* you could go?" Alex asked.

"I told my parents I'd go to the library right after school," Colin said sullenly. "My report on Jupiter is due tomorrow."

"Come on," Alex urged. "I'm supposed to be working on my report on Mars, but I'm blowing it off. You don't get a chance like this very often."

I wasn't going to be working on my report because

I had already finished it. So after school, I went home to shoot baskets in the driveway. Then I went in to play some video games. Just as I was taking off my socks, the phone rang, so I answered it.

"Hello?"

"Hey, Ten Toes!" said the caller. I could tell it was Alex. "Turn on the Channel 8 News!" Then he hung up.

I turned the TV to Channel 8. First, there was a story about a kid who was starting his own cookie business, but I soon realized it was the following story that Alex had wanted me to see:

"This is Leslie Vicar of Channel 8 News at the Acme Comic Book Store. Scores of Space Stuff fans have lined the sidewalks to meet one of the show's stars, Marv Martin. Let's talk to some of those who are waiting."

The reporter held her microphone in front of a kid in a Slugtop mask. I recognized the mask from the last time I was at the mall toy store. It looks like the head of a snail, with eyeballs on tentacles, and a big square mouth. But the coolest part is the distortion device that makes the wearer's voice sound like Slugtop's.

"Yeah, I should be working on a school paper," said the kid on the screen, in Slugtop's familiar robotic

drone. "But I wanted to meet my hero, Slugtop, the powerful warrior chief from the planet Zog."

"So, what is your name?" asked Leslie. "And what about Slugtop interests you so much?"

"Oh, yeah, my name is Colin Fredricks. And I'm not just into Space Stuff – I like stuff in space, too. Someday I hope to be the first astronaut to walk on Jupiter and plant an American flag on its surface."

I dashed to the phone and tried to call Colin, but the line was busy for a long time. I finally got through, but it was Colin's dad who answered. He told me he saw the TV news, and Colin wouldn't be talking on the phone, using his computer or having visitors for the next month. Colin would be on restriction, he said.

I talked to Colin the next day at school.

"Why'd you give your name on TV, Colin?" I asked. "You had the perfect disguise in that mask."

"It wasn't me, Nick. I went to the library, worked on my Jupiter report and turned it in today. I think that might have been Alex. He didn't want to get in trouble with his parents, so he said he was me."

"Okay, Colin, just come with me after school to see my friend, Bill. He can help straighten this all out."

"I can't go anywhere after school," said Colin.

"Remember? I'm on restriction."

"Okay, then I'll give you Bill's phone number, and you can call him."

"Can't. On restriction."

"E-mail?"

"Restriction."

"Maybe you can sneak out, Colin. After all, you're not guilty. You deserve a chance to prove it."

"Nick, my parents already think I'm lying. I'm not going to lie for real."

"Okay, but do you mind if I talk to Bill about the case?"

"Might as well," he said sadly.

I saw Bill after school. He listened as I told him about Colin's problem.

"Is there anyone at the library who might remember Colin was there?" Bill asked as he took notes.

"He doesn't think so."

"Did he check out any books? We could check the…"

"Check out and due dates? No, I thought of that. He used research books and didn't check out anything."

"I need to see that news story," Bill said. "Did anyone tape it?"

"I don't know, but I think we can see it at Channel 8's website."

Bill logged onto the News Center 8 website and found the Space Stuff story. After watching it, he said, "Let's go talk to this Alex kid."

I knocked on Alex's door and asked his dad if Alex could come out.

"Alex," Bill said, "I think it was you at the comic book store. I think when the reporter talked to you, you were afraid your parents would see you on TV and you figured you could lie about who you were because the mask would disguise your face and voice."

"Don't waste your breath, pig man," Alex said. "I have my parents fooled. They'll believe me, not some strange-looking warthog without evidence."

"Oh, I have evidence, Alex," Bill said. "But I think you could learn something from Colin. About the planets and the fifth commandment."

What evidence did Bill have? And what does the fifth commandment have to do with this?

 Turn to page 100 to find out!

# Chapter 7

# The Case of the Missing Birthday

Bill seemed to be enjoying my birthday party.

He won the three-legged race (as the only competitor who didn't need a partner), had the final piñata blow (with his tusks) and scarfed the cake and ice cream along with everyone else (especially with his side order of earthworms and rutabagas for toppings).

But after all the other guests had left, Bill was alone in the far corner of the lawn, nibbling on dandelions and looking rather sad.

"What's wrong, Bill?" I asked.

"I don't know, Nick. I had a lot of fun at the party and I appreciate your inviting me, but…"

"But what, Bill?"

"Whenever I go to a birthday party, it reminds me that I don't have a birthday."

"What do you mean? Everyone has a birthday."

"Oh, I know I have a birthday, Nick, but I don't know when it is. Remember what happened to me when I was young?"

I certainly did remember. When Bill had told me the story a few months earlier, I couldn't believe it.

Here's what happened, in Bill's own words:

"I was born in Africa. But poachers came when I was still a piglet and took me to the Pottersville Zoo.

"It was a horrible place. The cages were dirty and small. If it weren't for kids who shared their peanuts and popcorn, and the occasional stray cockroach, I would have starved.

"I was there for a month, but then this little girl, Shannon Thompson, saw me. She felt sorry for me, so when no one was looking she reached into the cage and took me. I was the runt of the litter, and could fit in her backpack.

"Shannon's parents didn't know about me until we got home. When she pulled me from her bag, they called the Department of Fish and Game. An official there said I was better off in their home than in the horror that is the Pottersville Zoo.

"So the Thompsons gave the zoo some money – they never told me how much   and filled out the forms for keeping a wild animal in their home. Can you imagine that I was once a wild animal?"

And that was the end of Bill's story. It explained a lot about how he came to be such a talented warthog.

Back at the party, I was stomping on balloons and Bill was popping them with his tusks.

"As I was growing up, we did celebrate the day I came home with Shannon," said Bill. "But I still don't know my actual birthday."

"But Bill, you're a detective. Can't you find that out?" I asked.

Two days later, Bill told me about his trip to the Pottersville Zoo. He took the bus, wearing his fedora, tie and trench coat disguise. He said the ticket seller gave him an odd look, but they never refused money at the Pottersville Zoo.

He said he went straight to the warthog cage, which was even smaller and dirtier than he remembered. But from the cage came excited grunts and squeals. He knew this sound.

Bill thought he recognized his brother's face. The other two looked familiar as well. He remembered that when Shannon had reached into the cage, the other warthogs had urged him to go with her.

Bill cried out, "Is that you, my brother? My friends?"

The warthogs were suddenly silent, looking at him with puzzled expressions. It seemed they didn't understand his English any more than he remembered his native warthog communication.

But as quickly as they had quieted, they suddenly burst into squeals. Bill turned to see a zookeeper with a net hovering over his head. Bill ran before the net came down.

And he didn't stop running until he reached the bus station and hid in a bathroom stall while he caught his breath. Then he called me and asked me to meet him in Pottersville.

"I'm going to need your help, Nick," he said. "I can't risk going back to that zoo, but we need to shut that place down. You'll need to go there with the proper authorities."

Bill set it all up. He called officials of the Department of Fish and Game, the Humane Society and

the FBI to meet me at the office of the Bosco brothers, owners of the Pottersville Zoo. Bill also set up a radio transmitter so he could hear everything that went on at the meeting, and I could hear him.

So there I was in the Pottersville Zoo office with three government officials, and Bob, Rob and Fernando Bosco.

Bob spoke first. "I appreciate you gentlemen from the government and animal relief agencies coming here out of concern for our animals. You may have heard that we don't care properly for our creatures, but I assure you we know everything about animals. Right, Rob?"

"Absolutely. I for one am spearheading an effort to breed black panthers and reintroduce them in the wild. Tell them what you're doing for the animals, Fernando."

Fernando said, "I'm working on a project to get every representative of the bear family here at our zoo: the brown bear, the black bear, the panda bear, the grizzly bear and the koala bear."

"You wouldn't want to stop great programs like

these," said Bob.

I heard Bill whisper in my receiver, "We've got all the evidence we need to nail these guys." And Bill told me what he meant.

I cleared my throat to get everyone's attention, then I said, "It looks like this zoo will be closing down. And if the three of you don't end up in cages, I'll be surprised."

Good homes were found for all the animals. Bill got to see his fellow warthogs before they were sent to a game preserve in Africa.

I met with Bill at his office a few weeks later.

"I'm glad we were able to get all of the animals to better homes, although I didn't accomplish what I set out to do," Bill said.

"You mean find your birthday?" I asked.

"Yeah," said Bill.

"I wouldn't be so sure about that. I made some calls and someone from the FBI sent me copies of paperwork from the Pottersville Zoo office. It seems the warthogs they had were estimated to have been born on February 2, Groundhog Day."

"Well, what do you know?" said Bill. "It'll be good to have a birthday to celebrate. You know, I think I'm beginning to understand the fourth commandment a little better."

What did the Bosco brothers say that showed they didn't know as much about animals as they claimed? And what is that fourth commandment?

 Turn to page 102 to find out!

# Chapter 8

# The Case of the Counterfeit Cookies

Charlie Palm's in my Sunday school class, so he's heard me talk about Bill. And Bill's always been a big fan of Charlie's. That's how I knew Bill would take the case when Charlie asked me.

After school one day, I took Charlie to Bill's office.

"Charlie, this is an honor," Bill said. "I love Charlie's Pretty Good Cookies."

Charlie is the only kid my age I know who has his own business. Well, I know kids who mow lawns and baby-sit. But Charlie makes cookies that everyone loves. A couple of local supermarkets even sell them.

After Bill asked us to sit down, Charlie began his story.

"I've had my cookie business for a year now," he said. "I've always liked baking, and I came up with a honey chocolate chip cookie recipe that my friends and family said was better than anything in the store.

"So I researched what it would take to start a business. My parents had our kitchen re-done to bring it up to the county health department's standards. And I got a business license.

"Then I started selling cookies in front of my house on a card table. Later, I found a factory that made cookie tins. And then I convinced a couple of local stores to sell my cookies, and they've been doing well."

"That's where I found your cookies," said Bill, "At the Piggly Wiggly. But I take it something has gone wrong."

Charlie nodded. "It started with a phone call. A woman complained about finding an eggshell in one of my cookies. I apologized and got her address so I could send her a free dozen.

"But then I got another call complaining about cookies that were bitter. And another about cookies that had too much flour. And another from someone who found a hair in a cookie."

Charlie looked exasperated. "I know I didn't make

those cookies," he said. "I have really strict quality control. I'm careful to use the same ingredients and procedures for every batch of cookies.

"Someone else must be selling cookies under my name. If word gets around about these bad cookie incidents, my business will be ruined."

As we got up to leave, Charlie handed Bill a piece of paper with the phone numbers of the complaining customers. Then Bill got to work.

As Bill made the calls, he quickly learned two interesting pieces of information:

1. The hair in the cookie was blonde (Charlie has dark hair).

2. All the complaining customers had purchased their cookies from a vending cart at the Elm Street Mall.

Bill and I took the bus to the mall. As we strolled in the door and gazed down the corridor, I couldn't believe what I saw: right in front of Game-a-Palooza (which is my favorite video game store, by the way), was a kid with a vending cart – hawking cookies!

"Excuse me, young man," said Bill as we approached him. "I take it you are selling cookies?"

The cart held several dozen tins bearing the name "Charlie's Pretty Good Cookies."

"What does it look like, tusk face?" said the kid, "Like I'm changing the oil in people's cars? You buying here or what?"

Bill looked peeved, but he remained professional. "Actually, I'm here as a representative of Charlie's Pretty Good Cookies. Have you been given authority to sell these cookies under Charlie's name?"

"Oh, there's nothing official," the kid shrugged. "I just went to the company that makes Charlie's tins and asked for some. They thought I worked for Charlie, so they sold me a hundred of 'em.

"I figured I'd expand Charlie's business some. After I made a good chunk of change, I was planning on using the phone number on the tin and giving Charlie a call with the good news that his business had grown. I was planning on sending half the profits to Charlie, but you can take it now if you want."

"Oh, I'm sure you were, Mr.…."

"Snidley. Brett Snidely."

"Brett, what you're doing is not right," Bill said. "Charlie is concerned about the good name of his company. You've been selling bad cookies using his

name, and it hurts his business."

"Oh, don't worry, I'm a great cook," said Brett. "A friend of a friend got Charlie's recipe for me. I'm making them exactly like he does. I have a photographic memory for recipes.

"And not only that, I have another amazing talent with recipes. I can just look at food and know how it will taste. And I have impeccable taste."

("'Impeccable' is a good thing," Bill whispered to me when he noticed my puzzled expression.)

"So," said Bill, "I could just show you a recipe, and you can tell whether it would turn out?"

"Sure," said Brett.

"Let me jot down an old recipe of Grandma Thompson's, and you tell me what you think," said Bill.

Bill pulled out a pencil and a 3" x 5" card, and wrote down the following recipe:

### Grandma Thompson's Ice Box Cookies

| | |
|---|---|
| 2 cups brown sugar | 1 spoon baking soda |
| 1/2 cup butter | 2 spoons vanilla |
| 2 eggs | 4 spoons ground walnuts |
| 3 1/2 cups flour | 1 spoon cream of tartar |

Mix and roll in loaf and freeze for two hours. Cut in slices and bake for 10 -12 minutes at 400 degrees. Cool for 10 minutes and serve.

"How would this recipe turn out?" Bill asked as he handed Brett the card.

Brett looked the card over. "These would be tasty cookies," he said, "though a bit dry for me. I've memorized all I need here."

"So, you know how to make Grandma Thompson's cookies?" Bill asked.

"Yep," said Brett. "I know all I need."

"And I know all I need to know," said Bill, "to prove you have a lot to learn about baking. You were missing key information, and yet you didn't even notice. I believe you owe an explanation and apology to the people to whom you sold cookies. And to Charlie, of course. You've been abusing the name of Charlie's Pretty Good Cookies, and it must stop."

Bill thought for a moment. "And this case reminds me why the third commandment is so important."

How did Bill figure out that Brett didn't know about baking? And what is the third commandment?

 Turn to page 104 to find out!

# Chapter 9

# The Case of the Talking Tree

Okay, so I was surprised to see the tree move. And I was surprised to see it stop about a block from my house and start to cry. After all, it wasn't a weeping willow – it looked like an elm.

But by the time I talked to it, I wasn't surprised it answered back.

"Excuse me, um, tree," I said. "I couldn't help noticing you moving, and, well, crying. You aren't really a tree, are you?"

Now I know you might think this was a stupid thing to ask, but when your best friend is a talking warthog, you become less sure about these things.

"Of course I'm not a tree, Ten Toes," said the tree.

"It's me, Elizabeth Tolbert, in the new school mascot costume."

"That is one convincing tree," I said. "But if you don't mind my asking, I could hear you crying. What was that all about?"

"You could hear me?" Elizabeth asked. "I was hoping the bark would muffle the sound. I was crying because someone has been sabotaging my costume, and I'm afraid that Principal Kingstone will make someone else the school mascot."

"Who's been sabotaging the costume, Elizabeth?"

"I don't know," she said. "I've been bringing home the costume after school to work on halftime routines. I leave it in the garage when I'm done. But then when I go back to get it, someone has sawed off the branches!"

"Can't you bring it back to school? Or leave it in the house instead of the garage?" I asked.

"I need to work on the routines at home," she answered. "And it won't fit in the house. But whoever is doing this has already sawed off eight branches."

"When do you think the limbs are being sawed?"

"I think usually while my family is eating dinner."

I called Bill and asked him if he could do a

stakeout at Elizabeth's to see who was sawing off the branches. He said he was swamped with paperwork, but he thought it was a job that I could handle.

I called my parents, and they said I could stay at Elizabeth's and help out. She suggested I hide in the rafters in the garage, so she set up the ladder and helped me up there.

I didn't have to wait long. About 10 minutes into Elizabeth's dinner, I saw a strange creature come in through the garage doggie door: a giant beaver.

Well, it was about 5 feet tall, but for a beaver that would be giant! After it spotted the tree, it started to chew off a branch with its huge front teeth.

I should have reacted more quickly, but this was all pretty weird, even for a guy with a warthog friend. Finally, as it started to saw another branch, I shouted, "Stop!"

The beaver knocked down the ladder – stranding me in the rafters – and crawled back out the doggie door. There was no safe way down, so I had to wait until Elizabeth's family heard my embarrassed cries.

After Mr. Tolbert put the ladder back, I climbed down, went home and called Bill.

"A giant beaver, you say?" asked Bill after I told

him my story. "Originally I suspected someone from your school who might want to take Elizabeth's place as mascot, but not now."

"What are you thinking, Bill?"

"Are there any schools that use a beaver as a mascot?"

"Of course," I said. "Bay City Elementary."

"I think I'll be handling the rest of this case on my own," said Bill. "But I do have one more question for you, Nick. Was there sawdust at the crime scene?"

"Yeah, all over the place. Why do you ask?"

"I hope I can explain it all, after I wrap up this case."

I went to Bill's office Saturday afternoon. He looked rather pleased with himself as he told me the rest of the story.

"After I heard your report, Nick, I did an Internet search and found that a sixth-grade student, Garrett Morten, wears the beaver mascot suit for Bay City Elementary. So I looked up his address.

"This morning, I took a bus to Bay City, but I had to walk a ways to the Mortens' house. It is out in the country, down in a canyon. It's a cube of a house with a flat roof, and only a satellite dish and gravel on top.

"I knocked at the door, and Garrett answered in his beaver suit. He said, 'Hey, you must be the mascot for the Watsonville Warthogs! Great costume!'

"I didn't contradict him. I said, 'That's quite a costume you've got on, Garrett.'

"And Garrett said, 'Thanks,' and flapped his large flat tail. When he did that, I noticed some sawdust on his costume. Then he said, 'I like to wear my costume all through the sports season. It keeps up that Beaver spirit.'

"I was looking at Garrett's mouth while he was talking. He has enormous sharp teeth! So I asked if he

 could actually cut wood with them. And he said yes, that the costume could be 'real useful.' He told me the original wooden teeth kept breaking, so he made new teeth using saw blades.

"Then I told him that someone's been sabotaging costumes, particularly the costume for Elm Street Elementary, and that I couldn't help noticing the sawdust on his costume.

"'He said he'd heard that someone had been sabotaging other schools' costumes, but it wasn't him.

Then he said a couple of weird things. First, he said, 'Who wouldn't want do whatever they could to make sure their school mascot was the best?' And he said, 'As for the sawdust, it's been getting cold so I've been sawing firewood for the fireplace.'

"So I said, 'Garrett, I'm afraid you've just told me who's been sabotaging Elizabeth Tolbert's costume. You've made this costume of yours an idol. You're going to have to pay to repair Elizabeth's costume, and stop idolizing your costume.'"

"How could you be sure he was lying, Bill?" I asked.

"You've seen me work long enough, Nick," said Bill. "I've told you what you need to know to figure out this case. I'm just hoping I told Garrett enough so he'll follow the second commandment."

How was Bill sure Garrett was lying? And what is the second commandment?

 Turn to page 106 to find out!

# Chapter 10

# The Case of the Moses Mystery

Unless Bill cuts down on those mealworm and lawn-clipping tacos before bed, he's going to keep having bizarre dreams. Here's a dream he told me recently:

Before bed, I was reading in Exodus where God leads the Israelites out of slavery in Egypt and into the wilderness. So it wasn't surprising that I dreamed about that very thing.

I was looking out over a desert landscape and saw thousands of people milling around some tents. I spoke to a young, dark-skinned boy grinding some kind of grain with a mortar and pestle.

(A sure sign that this was a dream was that everyone spoke English!)

"What are you making, young man?" I asked.

"Manna cakes," the boy responded. "It's just about all we eat; people say in Egypt we used to eat all kinds of things. My parents say manna is a miracle provided by God every morning, and we should be thankful for it."

Then I noticed I was surrounded by men with spears.

"Look at this creature," said one man. "I bet there's a lot of meat on those bones."

"I'm so tired of manna," said another. "It'll be good to have some meat besides quail."

"Whoever makes the killing blow gets the pork chops!" exclaimed a third.

I looked for the friendly face of the young boy, but he was nowhere to be seen.

"You're making a mistake," I cried. "If I wake up, you'll be gone!"

"The creature speaks!" called one of them.

But another man stepped forward. "I don't care if he speaks or flies! I'm hungry, and this spear will silence him."

The man lifted his spear in the air.

"You will do no such thing, Dathan," said a man as he grabbed the end of Dathan's spear.

"This is no business of yours, Eldad," the one called "Dathan" whined.

"But it is the business of all our people to avoid meat that God calls unclean. The Law says you may not eat any animal that splits the hoof and does not chew its cud," he said.

"But look, Eldad, it is chewing its cud like a cow," said Dathan.

I quickly spit out my Juicy Fruit gum. "He's right," I said. "I am, thankfully, unclean to eat under your laws."

"All right, pig. I'll deal with you later," Dathan said as he stalked away.

"Thanks for stepping in, Eldad," I said.

"Don't thank me, but rather Benjamin here. He told me you were in trouble."

The boy stepped forward, grinning. Eldad walked away.

"Thank you, Benjamin," I said. "If I can ever be of

help to you, let me know. My name's Bill."

"I doubt you can help me. My problem is with Dathan."

"Could you tell me about it?"

"Some days ago, God gave instructions for building His tabernacle, a moving temple. He asked for everyone to contribute treasures we brought from Egypt. Our family doesn't have much, but we did have some lumber, which is rare here in the desert.

"So we took the acacia wood to Bezalel and Oholiab, who were collecting the materials, but after dropping it off, we heard they had more than enough to build the tabernacle. When I went to see about getting the wood back, Dathan said it was his instead."

"What were you going to do with the wood, Benjamin?" I asked.

"I hoped to build a wagon to help my family carry our goods," he said.

"So how is this dispute going to be settled?"

"It is our system, Bill, to bring disputes first to the leaders of tens, then leaders of hundreds, then leaders of thousands," said Benjamin. "But we did that already. And since none of those leaders could find a solution, today we see Moses himself."

"I know I'm a stranger, Benjamin," I said, "but may I come with you?"

Benjamin agreed. We walked a ways and came to a brightly-colored tent with a whole bunch of people waiting outside. Then we saw Dathan.

"So you came, crybaby, and brought your walking supper with you," the large man taunted.

"Of course Benjamin came, Dathan," I said defiantly. "But why won't you give him the wood that's rightfully his?"

"It's my wood, pig, and I have plans for it," Dathan said.

I tried not to get my hooves in a twist. "Technically speaking," I said, "I'm a warthog. And what are your plans?"

"I need a new walking stick, and my wife wants a jewelry box," said Dathan. "And we'd both like new stools. Better plans than the toys this brat would make."

"My wagon will be a tool, not a toy, Dathan," said Benjamin.

Dathan sneered and turned his back on us. We then were called into Moses' tent.

Moses was a grand figure in a long robe with a long

white beard. But it was his brother Aaron who spoke.

"This case regards acacia wood not needed for construction of the tabernacle," Aaron called out. "You may speak first, young man."

Benjamin stepped up to the front. "Thank you, Moses and Aaron, for hearing my case. My family does not have much, but we brought what we had. We hoped the wood might be used to build the tabernacle, but since it was not needed for that, we hoped to use it for a wagon for our travels. I trust in your wisdom for this decision."

"And you, Dathan?" Aaron said.

Benjamin took a few steps back while Dathan came to the front.

"Moses, Aaron," he said. "It is an honor to tell you that I was happy to bring wood for the tabernacle. In fact, I had already brought everything of value my family had. All our gold, silver and fine jewels had been accepted for construction. Is it so much to receive back a few pieces of wood to make a gift for my wife?"

There was silence, but I knew I had to say something.

"I know I am a stranger here, but may I say

something?" I asked.

Moses motioned me to him, and I whispered in his ear. He then stood and spoke.

"I rule in favor of Benjamin. The wood is his," said Moses. "Dathan, you have broken several of the commandments that the Lord has given us. You have coveted, lied and tried to steal. If you learn to follow the first commandment, all the others will fall in place. If not, your future is dim."

Just then, I woke up happy. Even if it was just a dream, I knew justice had been served.

What evidence did Bill give Moses? And what is the first commandment?

Turn to page 108 to find out!

# The Case of the Vanishing Video Game

**Q:** *How did Bill know Hurley wasn't telling the truth?*

**A:** Hurley said the power at his house had been off for half an hour, and that it had just come back on. But the digital clock still had the correct time.

When Bill confronted him with this fact, Hurley admitted he was jealous of Nick's video game system, and he had been shutting off the power at Nick's house so Nick couldn't enjoy his game. But Hurley apologized to Nick. And now his parents let him play games at Nick's house most weekends.

**Q:** *What does the last commandment have to do with this story?*

**A:** The Ten Commandments are the laws God gave to Moses for the people of Israel. The Ten Commandments are the basis of modern law. (You can find them in the Bible in Exodus 20 and Deuteronomy 5.)

The last commandment says, "You shall not covet your neighbor's wife, house, servant, ox, or donkey or anything that belongs to your neighbor, including his video game system."

Okay, I added the video game part. But to covet is to be jealous of something that belongs to someone else – to want something so much that you don't want to see anyone else enjoy it. As Hurley discovered, coveting only leads to trouble. That's why God wants us to be happy with what we have, and avoid jealousy.

# The Case of the Too-Good-to-Be-True Travels

**Q:** *What did Katie say that Bill could prove wasn't true?*

**A:** First of all, Bill said it was "about time" that Katie told the truth. He chose those words carefully to make a point: she didn't tell the truth about time. She said she left New York City after a noon lunch and the flight got her to Paris by 6 p.m.

That isn't possible! Although there are jets that can travel that distance in four hours, you have to calculate the time zones you cross to figure out what time it will be when you arrive. For example, when it's 6 p.m. in New York, it's midnight in Paris. So even if Katie and her dad had somehow taken a supersonic jet, Katie would have reached Paris in time for bed, not dinner!

But that's not all. Katie's photo of herself holding the Mona Lisa, which touched from her chin to her toes, made the famous painting appear large, when it is really quite small. And she could not have left flowers at the grave of the Hunchback of Notre Dame because there is no such place – the Hunchback is a fictional character!

**Q:** *What is the ninth commandment that Bill mentioned?*

**A:** Exodus 20:16 says "You shall not bear false witness," which means you shouldn't lie. But this isn't the only place the Bible urges people to tell the truth. Ephesians 4:15 tells us to "speak the truth in love." We shouldn't even be telling "white lies" that supposedly don't hurt anyone.

When Bill revealed the facts, Katie apologized to the other students. She had wanted to be president so much that she was willing to lie to win. So she lost the election, but she did agree to help President Tito with the camping trip.

# The Case of the Quiz Show Questions

**Q:** *How did Bill know that Cody was guilty? And what exactly does that last spelling word mean?*

**A:** Bill's instincts made him suspicious of Cody's accusations against Thor, but Cody's answers provided the evidence.

The third vocabulary question (which Bill did not read) was "What is the material for writing letters?" The answer was "stationery." But there is a word that sounds just the same: "stationary," which means "staying in one place." Cody didn't ask which word Bill wanted him to spell.

The next question was the one that really convinced Bill that Cody was guilty: "What word means a basic rule or law that sounds like Mr. Kingstone's title?"

The answer was "principle," but, again, there is a word that sounds just the same: "principal."

Because they were standing by the principal's

office, it would have been likely that Cody would choose that spelling. Unless Cody had seen the answer sheet.

**Q:** *What is the eighth commandment?*

**A:** Bill knew Cody was guilty of larceny (which means theft), breaking the eighth commandment ("You shall not steal")

When we think of stealing, we often think of robbery or shoplifting. But cheating on a test in school is stealing answers and breaking this commandment. Cody confessed to the principal, and got detention. Thor used his winnings to treat Bill, Nick and Skip to burritos at the snack bar.

# The Case of the Multiplying Pets

**Q:** *How was Bill sure the pets belonged to Dennis?*

**A:** Bill knew Dennis was lying. He referred to the puppy as "her" and the kitten as "he." That is probably the least typical way to identify the pets if he didn't know them (he most likely would have called them "it").

Dennis admitted he had kept each of the pets for a week, but then got bored with them. He didn't want to do the work to take care of them. He knew Danielle's family was responsible and would take care of the pets when he didn't want to bother with them anymore.

Bill told Dennis that when we take in pets, it's our responsibility to care for them. If Dennis wanted to have a pet, Bill said, he should commit to being responsible for it.

Bill told Dennis that the excitement of having a new pet would wear off, but that might be when a real friendship begins.

**Q:** *And what is the seventh commandment?*

**A:** The seventh commandment says, "You shall not commit adultery." That means that in marriage, a man and woman should stick together and be faithful to each other.

Marriage is a much bigger commitment than getting a pet. But God wants us to take all of our responsibilities seriously, even those we have as kids. Learning responsibility now will help us be ready for the exciting possibilities God has for us when we grow up.

# The Case of the Raccoon Twins

**Q:** *What question could Bill have asked to solve the mystery?*

**A:** The question Bill could have asked one of the Raccoon Brothers is, "Who would your brother say threw the chair?" He could ask this of either raccoon. The truthful brother would tell the truth about his brother's lie. And if Bill asked the lying brother about the honest brother's truth, the lying brother would lie. So for either brother, the answer to the question of "who would your brother say threw the chair?" would be the opposite of the truth. If either brother answered, "My brother would say the fox threw the chair," for instance, Bill would know that the wolverine threw the chair.

Not that it really matters whether the fox or the wolverine threw the chair because, remember, it was just a dream.

**Q:** *What is the sixth commandment, and what did Bill mean by saying he had broken it in the "broadest sense"?*

**A:** The sixth commandment is "You shall not murder." Most people don't worry about breaking this

commandment. But Jesus said in Matthew 5:21-22 that we are breaking this commandment even when we are just unkind to others.

Bill knew that in the dream he had been angry and insulting toward Sergeant Weasel. If it had been real life, rather than a dream, those things would be sins.

It is good to know God forgives our sins when we confess them to Him (as you can read in the Bible in 1 John 1:9), even if we are mean to a brother, sister or friend. Not only can you ask the other person for forgiveness, but you can ask God, and know He will forgive you.

# The Case of the Space Mask

**Q:** *What evidence did Bill have?*

**A:** Bill had the evidence he needed when he heard the kid on the TV interview say "walk on Jupiter and plant an American flag on its surface."

Jupiter is a gaseous planet, and there is no surface on which to walk or set a flag. Colin, who was very interested in space, had been working on a report about Jupiter. He wouldn't have made that mistake in the interview.

Alex called Nick before the interview was even broadcast. He was the most obvious suspect.

**Q:** *What does the fifth commandment have to do with this?*

**A:** The fifth commandment is "Honor your father and mother." Alex was not obeying this commandment when he tried to fool his parents about going to the comic book store. Colin obeyed his parents, even when, in this case, they were wrong.

God gives us parents to take care of us and teach us how to live. We are to obey them while we are under their authority. When we grow up, we aren't called to obey them, but we are always to honor them.

A key part of honoring our parents is to be honest with them. This commandment comes with a promise that if we honor our parents, we will have long lives, and things will go well for us.

Alex learned what the fifth commandment was, and a month-long restriction from his parents helped him learn to practice it. Colin's parents took away his restriction, and even treated him and Nick to a trip to the planetarium that weekend.

# The Case of the Missing Birthday

**Q:** *What did the Bosco brothers say that showed they didn't know as much about animals as they claimed?*

**A:** The government officials were inclined to be suspicious of the Bosco brothers, but what Bob, Rob and Fernando said convinced everyone these brothers were not knowledgeable about animals.

Rob said he had a program to reintroduce "black panthers" to the wild. There is no such species. Some leopards are just darker than others.

Fernando claimed he wanted representatives of all the bear family, but koalas and pandas aren't really bears. Koalas are marsupials, like kangaroos. Pandas are more closely related to raccoons.

**Q:** *What is that fourth commandment?*

**A:** The fourth commandment is "Remember the Sabbath day and keep it holy." Just as we pay special attention to people on their birthdays, this commandment says we should pay special attention to God one day a week.

God had the Jews use Saturday as that special day of honor to Him. Most Christians now set aside Sunday to honor God, in remembrance of Jesus' resurrection on Easter Sunday.

God didn't just give this commandment so that He would be honored (although He deserves that honor), but also because He knew we would need the rest this special day brings.

# The Case of the Counterfeit Cookies

**Q:** *How did Bill figure out that Brett didn't know about baking?*

**A:** Brett revealed that he was not a good baker when he claimed that the recipe Bill showed him had all the information he needed.

The recipe Bill wrote read, "1 spoon baking soda, 2 spoons vanilla, 4 spoons ground walnuts, 1 spoon cream of tartar." It didn't specify the kinds of spoons that should be used. Recipes usually specify tablespoons (larger) or teaspoons (smaller). Most likely, the baking soda, vanilla and cream of tartar would have been measured in teaspoons, and the walnuts in a tablespoon.

Brett didn't have the information he needed, but he thought he was ready to make the cookies anyway. He was not the cook he thought he was. He certainly had no right to be using the name of Charlie's Pretty Good Cookies.

**Q:** *What is the third commandment?*

**A:** Bill referred to the third commandment, which says, "You shall not use God's name in vain." Names  are important. This commandment says we should not misuse God's name. There are people who use God's name when they hit their thumbs with hammers. There are people who say Jesus' name when they are mad or frustrated.

But there are other ways we can misuse God's name, too. When we call ourselves Christians, but do not act like Christ, we are misusing His name. When we say things about God that aren't true, we're misusing His name.

He does want us to use His name, though...to talk to Him. So don't misuse it, but do use it.

# The Case of the Talking Tree

**Q:** *How was Bill sure Garrett was lying?*

**A:** Bill didn't believe Garrett's denial for many reasons. For one thing, there aren't a lot of five-foot tall beavers running around. But more important was the sawdust on the beaver costume, which Bill suspected was from the Elm costume.

Garrett said he had been sawing firewood. But as you'll recall, Bill saw the roof of Garrett's house, and it was flat. There was a satellite dish, but no chimney or stovepipe.

And if there was no chimney, there was no fireplace, and Garrett was not sawing firewood.

Garrett admitted he had sabotaged Elizabeth's costume and agreed to pay to repair it.

**Q:** *What is the second commandment?*

**A:** The second commandment is "You shall not make for yourself an idol…You shall not bow down or worship them."

Garrett had made his beaver costume, and maybe his school (believe it or not), into an idol. In Moses'  time (and in some parts of the world today), people worshipped actual statue idols. But all of us at times put "idols" before God. An idol can be anything you put above God in your life, whether it's video games, sports or music.

We need to love God first, as He loves us.

# The Case of the Moses Mystery

**Q:** *What evidence did Bill give Moses?*

**A:** The evidence Bill brought Moses was from something Dathan said. Outside the tent, Dathan said he was going to make a jewelry box for his wife. But inside the tent he said he had given all his gold, silver, fine jewels and everything else of value for the building of the tabernacle.

If Dathan really had given everything of value, there would be nothing to put in that jewelry case.

This mystery was just Bill's dream, of course. But there really were men named Dathan and Eldad, and they are mentioned in the Bible's story of the Israelites' travels through the wilderness, in the book of Numbers. And, of course, Aaron and Moses were real people, too. Through Moses, God gave the Ten Commandments to the people of Israel, and to us all.

**Q:** *What is the first commandment?*

**A:** The first commandment is "You shall have no other gods before me." If Dathan had put God first in his life, instead of his greed, he would have stayed out of trouble.

 When we put other things before our relationship with God, we eventually end up sinning, and breaking all the commandments. But God sent His Son, Jesus, to die on the cross and make right the things we've done wrong.

All you need to do is ask God to forgive your sins, and He will. Then you can put God first in your life by giving your life to Him. You still will do wrong things at times, but you can do better with God's Spirit working in you.

# "Crime is like a cockroach, but not as tasty."

## – Bill the Warthog

Get more Bill with *Full Metal Trench Coat*, the first book in the **Bill the Warthog Mysteries** series. Can you solve the crimes for Nick and his friends before Bill does?

ISBN 10: 1-58411-068-6
ISBN 13: 978-1-58411-068-2

# The fun devotionals that help you grow closer to God.

*Gotta Have God* (for guys) and *God and Me!* (for girls) are packed with over 100 devotionals each, plus memory verses, stories, journal space and fun activities to help you learn more about the Bible.

**Gotta Have God for Guys 10-12, Vol. 1**
ISBN 1-885358-98-9

**Gotta Have God for Guys 10-12, Vol. 2**
ISBN 1-58411-059-7

**God and Me! for Girls 10-12, Vol. 1**
ISBN 1-885358-54-7

**God and Me! for Girls 10-12, Vol. 2**
ISBN 1-58411-056-2